DISNEY · PIXAR
COCO

SING YOUR SONG

This book belongs to

....

This edition published by Parragon Books Ltd in 2017 and distributed by

Parragon Inc.
440 Park Avenue South, 13th Floor
New York, NY 10016
www.parragon.com

Written and edited by Charlie Wilson   Designed by Joanne Eyre

ISBN 978-1-4748-9105-9

Printed in China

DISNEY · PIXAR
COCO

SING YOUR SONG

PaRragon

Bath • New York • Cologne • Melbourne • Delhi
Hong Kong • Shenzhen • Singapore

MIGUEL IS A LITTLE BOY WITH A BIG DREAM.

Imagine your own great adventure and draw it here.

Spend time with your loved ones and create your own FAMILY TREE. Take time together to fill in the pages and share stories. You might learn more about yourself, too—like where your love of music comes from.

Add your picture here

Paste in a picture of yourself at the bottom and move upward.

MAMÁ IMELDA,

Miguel's great-great-grandmother banned music from the family.

  Write down any rules your parents set for you.

 Now write down any rules you would like to set for your parents!

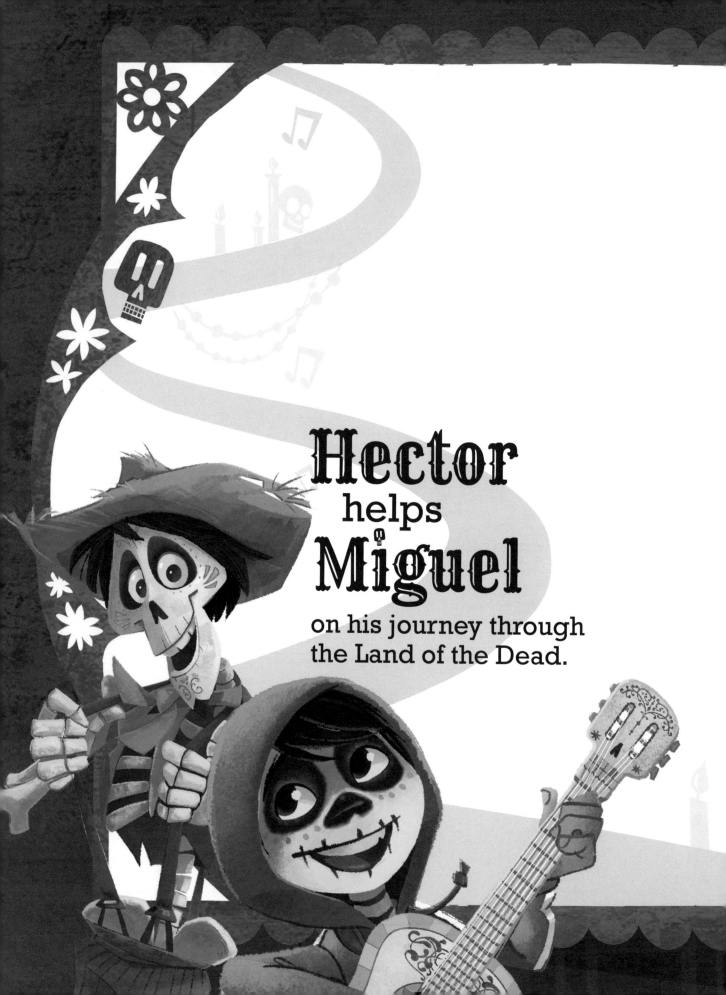

Hector
helps
Miguel
on his journey through
the Land of the Dead.

Draw you and your friends on an **exciting adventure together.**

"THE REST OF THE WORLD MAY FOLLOW THE RULES, BUT I MUST FOLLOW MY HEART." Ernesto de la Cruz

Use your **imagination** and draw the LAND OF THE DEAD …

...then add some MYSTICAL CREATURES...

...and
SKELETONS
to your picture.

♪ ♫ Miguel never feels more alive than when he's playing his guitar. ♪♫

Draw a picture of yourself doing your favorite hobby or activity.

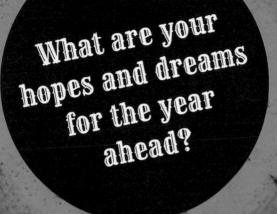

What are your hopes and dreams for the year ahead?

Write about something new you'd like to do each month in this planner—then seize your moment and make your DREAMS a reality!

January

February

March

April

May

June

July

August

September

October

November

December

SEIZE YOUR

MOMENT

We all see the world differently.
Draw exciting scenes seen
through the eyes of
each skull.

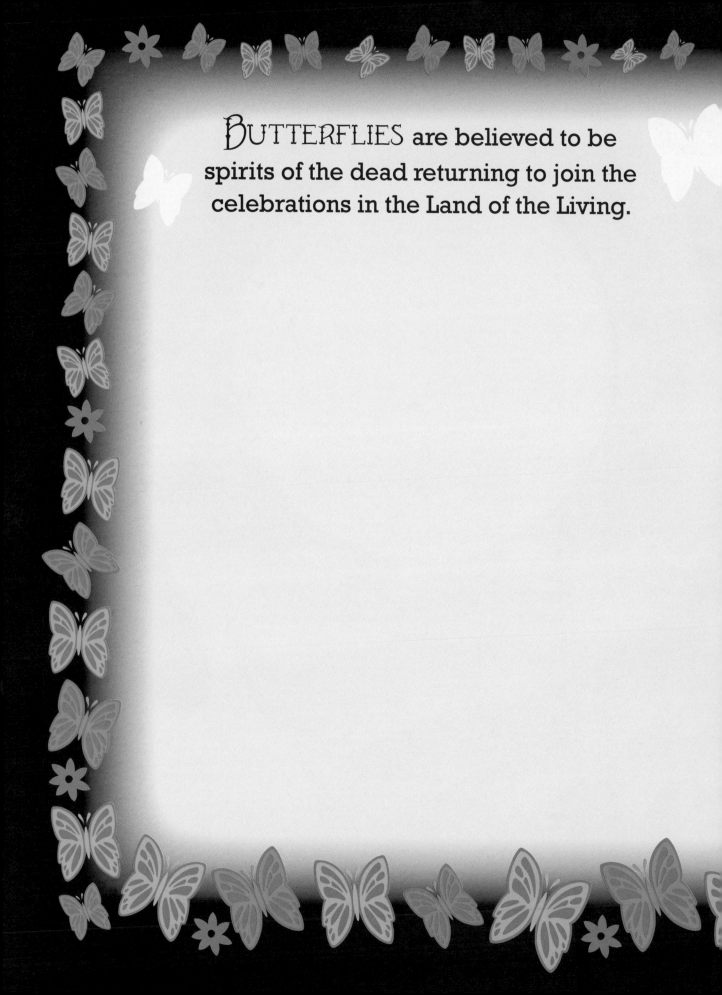

BUTTERFLIES are believed to be spirits of the dead returning to join the celebrations in the Land of the Living.

Draw fluttering butterflies.

Color their wings with bright, festive colors.

Miguel's family believes that whatever road we choose in life, it's always a little easier in a new pair of shoes.

Write about your next journey here.

Leaving from:

Traveling to:

Transportation:

Describe your journey in three words:

Draw a picture of your dream destination.

Write down the names of all the places
you'd love to visit one day.

The Land of the Dead
isn't dark—it shines!

Fill the page with light by coloring in the candles and drawing more.

The LAND OF THE DEAD is full of magical creatures called spirit animals.

Draw your own **spirit animal.**

Design your own
papel picado
banners for a fiesta of fun.

Draw the things you love, or memories from your favorite celebrations.

It's important to remember your
family and friends.

Draw or write about a
happy memory
you have shared with
your loved ones.

The smell of the marigolds is believed to guide the souls of the dead back to the Land of the Living.

Fill this page with beautiful marigolds.

IN LIFE, WE ALL DANCE TO OUR OWN BEAT.

Draw a picture of yourself **dancing** and having fun!

Use your colors to bring this page to life!

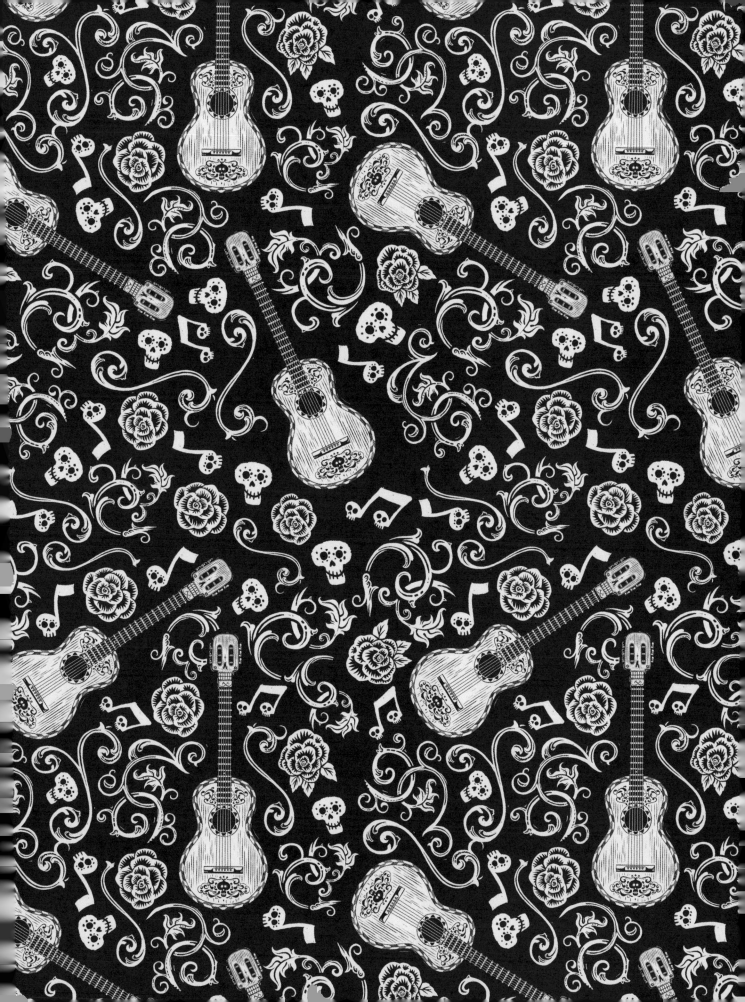

ADVENTURE
LIGHTS THE WAY!

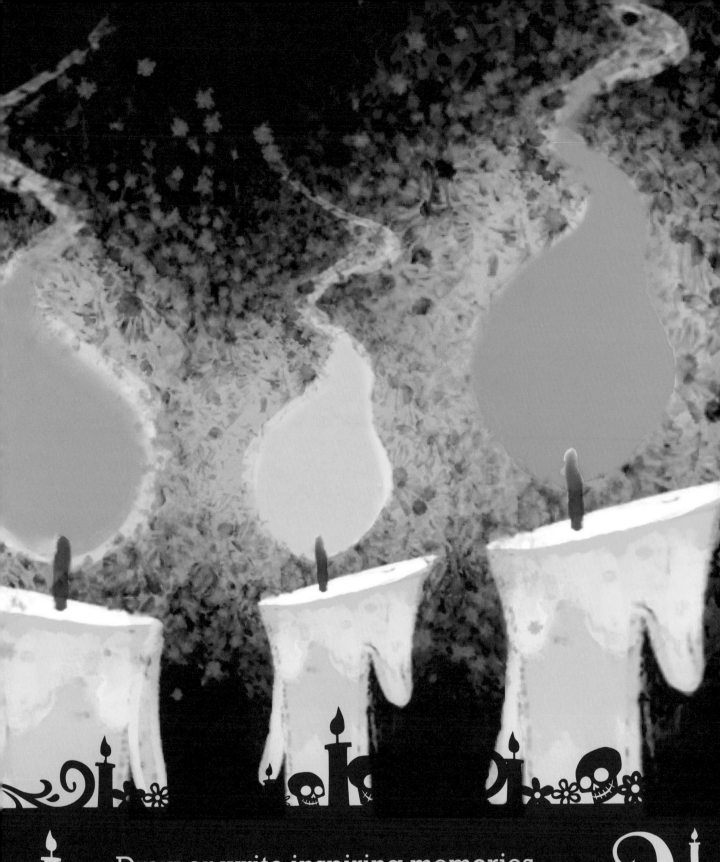

Draw or write inspiring memories
and thoughts in the flames to help
guide you on your journey.

The skeletons are performing the
DANCE OF THE DEAD
—they're the life of the party!

Draw a **bony body** under each **skull.**

MIGUEL'S favorite instrument is the guitar.

Can you draw other exciting instruments for him to play?

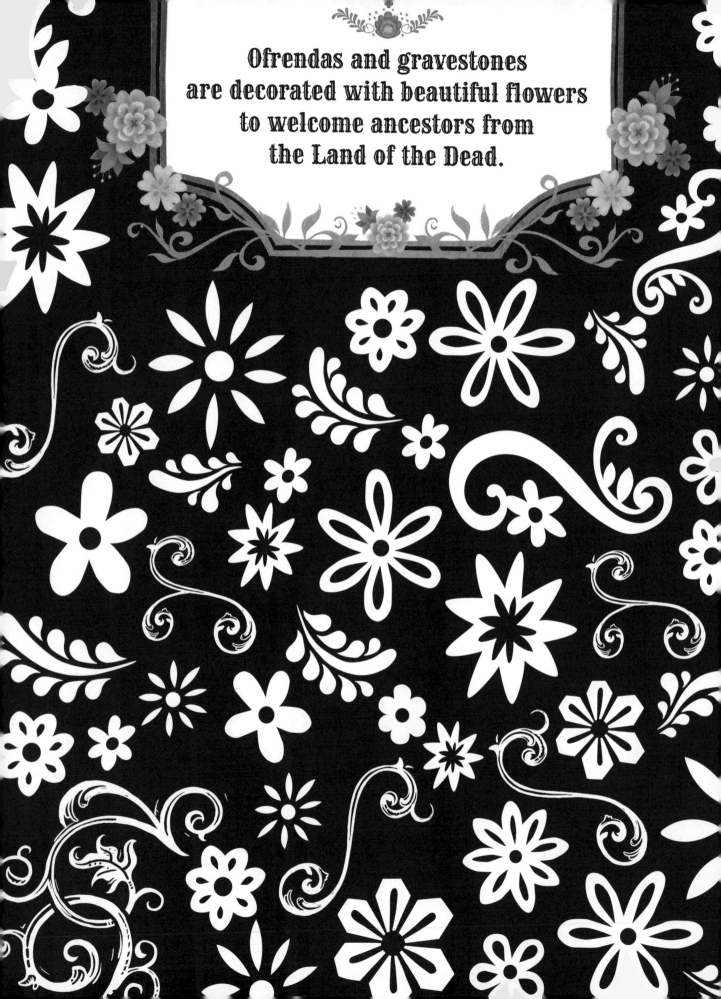

Ofrendas and gravestones
are decorated with beautiful flowers
to welcome ancestors from
the Land of the Dead.

Breathe new life
into this page with color.

Miguel enjoys writing songs.
He's scribbled some ideas for lyrics
below ... add some more.

DANCE TO YOUR OWN BEAT

THE RHYTHM OF LIFE

SEIZE THE MOMENT

A SONG HAS THE POWER TO CHANGE A HEART

THE FORGOTTEN FADE FROM THE LAND OF THE DEAD WHEN NO ONE REMEMBERS THEM.

Draw or write all the special things you want people to remember about you.

Creativity can GROW from the

Each time you have a creative thought,
write or draw it in one of the flowers
and watch your ideas blossom.

most **unexpected** places.

Use this page to store
all your ideas.

Add some mystical designs to the sugar skull mask, and then color it in. Fill this page with lots more colorful skulls to liven it up!

We meet many special people on our journey through life.

Use these pages to draw and write about friends, family, and loved ones who inspire you.

A graveyard can be
a SCARY place.

Draw flowers and SKELETONS DANCING
to make this somber scene more welcoming.

The celebrations begin at night when the dead return to the Land of the Living. Draw the moon high in the sky.

The festival ends when the sun goes down.
Now draw a beautiful sunset.

Miguel has so many dreams and ambitions. He wants to explore and share his music with the world . . . one day!

Use these pages to imagine YOUR future.

Draw a portrait of yourself twenty years from now.

What job will you have?

Where do you want to be living twenty years from now?

☐ On a remote mountain

☐ In an exotic country

☐ In a friendly town

☐ By the ocean

Which of these predictions do you think will come true for you? Twenty years from now . . .

☐ I will be famous

☐ I will have climbed a mountain

☐ I will still have the same best friend

☐ I will have seen the sunrise in a far-off land

Write a letter to your future self below.
Then cut along the solid lines and fold along the dotted lines.
Close your letter and store it somewhere safe.
Open it years from now to remember the amazing younger you!

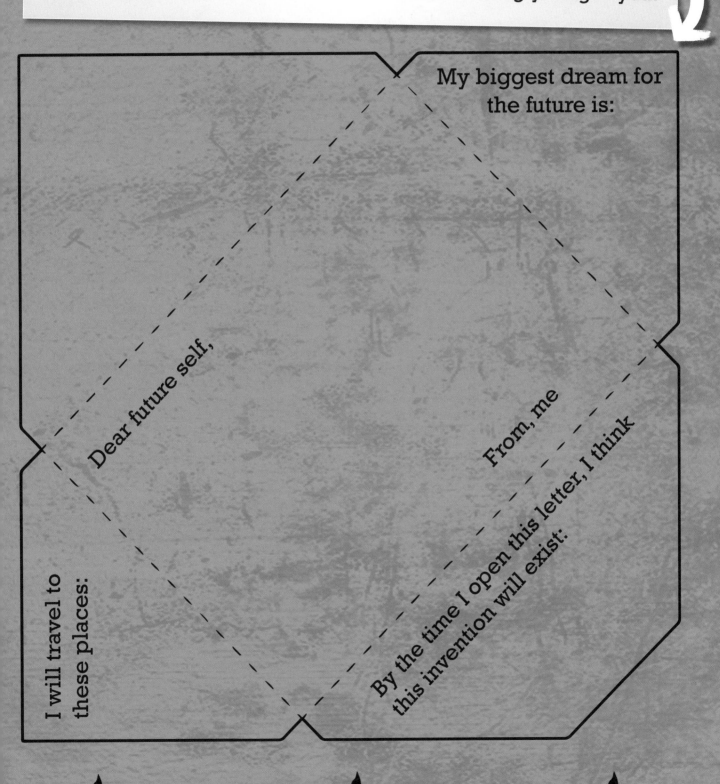

My biggest dream for the future is:

Dear future self,

From, me

By the time I open this letter, I think this invention will exist:

I will travel to these places:

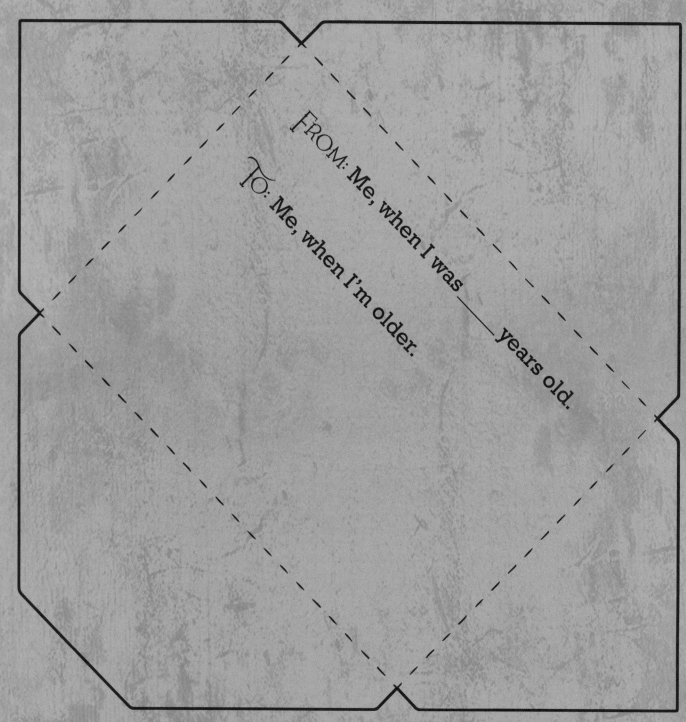

From: Me, when I was _____ years old.

To: Me, when I'm older.